Story Time with Signs & Rhymes

The Big Blue Bowl
Sign Language for Food

by Dawn Babb Prochovnic
illustrated by Stephanie Bauer

Content Consultant:
William Vicars, EdD, Director of Lifeprint Institute
and Associate Professor, ASL & Deaf Studies
California State University, Sacramento

magic wagon

visit us at www.abdopublishing.com

For my friend Kate, a most welcome guest at my table—DP
To Dawn – Thanks for such fabulous words to illustrate!—SB

Printed in the United States.

 PRINTED ON RECYCLED PAPER

Written by Dawn Babb Prochovnic
Illustrations by Stephanie Bauer
Edited by Stephanie Hedlund and Rochelle Baltzer
Cover and Interior design by Neil Klinepier

Story Time with Signs & Rhymes provides an introduction to ASL vocabulary through stories that are written and structured in English. ASL is a separate language with its own structure. Just as there are personal and regional variations in spoken and written languages, there are similar variations in sign language.

Library of Congress Cataloging-in-Publication Data
Prochovnic, Dawn Babb.
  The big blue bowl : sign language for food / by Dawn Babb Prochovnic ; illustrated by Stephanie Bauer; content consultant, William Vicars.
    p. cm. -- (Story time with signs & rhymes)
  Includes "alphabet handshapes;" American Sign Language glossary, fun facts, and activities; further reading and web sites.
  ISBN 978-1-60270-668-2
  [1. Stories in rhyme. 2. Food--Fiction. 3. American Sign Language. 4. Vocabulary.] I. Bauer, Stephanie, ill. II. Title.
  PZ8.3.P93654Big 2009
  [E]--dc22
                    2009002400

Alphabet Handshapes

American Sign Language (ASL) is a visual language that uses handshapes, movements, and facial expressions. Sometimes people spell English words by making the handshape for each letter in the word they want to sign. This is called fingerspelling. The pictures below show the handshapes for each letter in the manual alphabet.

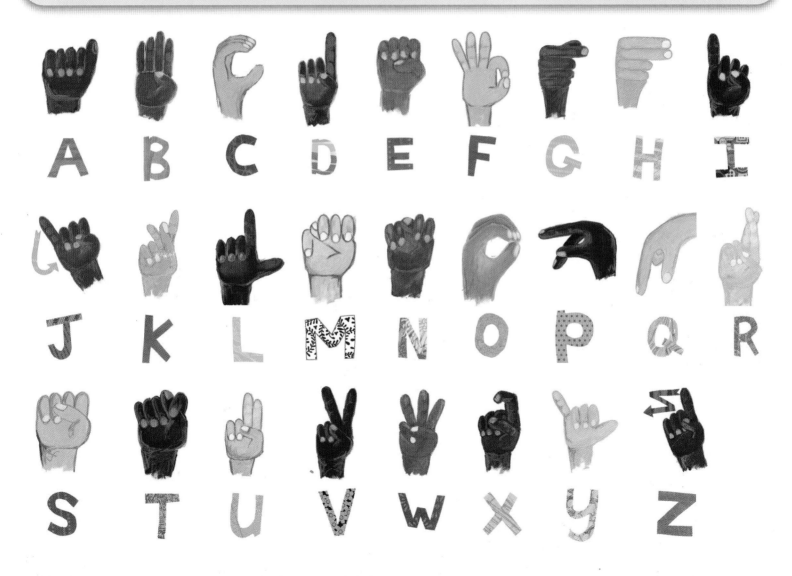

There is a **bowl** in front of me. It is the biggest **bowl** that you ever did see. It's a big blue **bowl**.

"Fill it up, fill it up, fill it up," I say. And my friends fill it up with me.

bowl

Duck piles **beans** into our bowl. They are the heartiest **beans** that you
ever did see. The **beans** go in the big blue bowl.
  "Fill it up, fill it up, fill it up," I say. And my friend Duck fills it up with me.

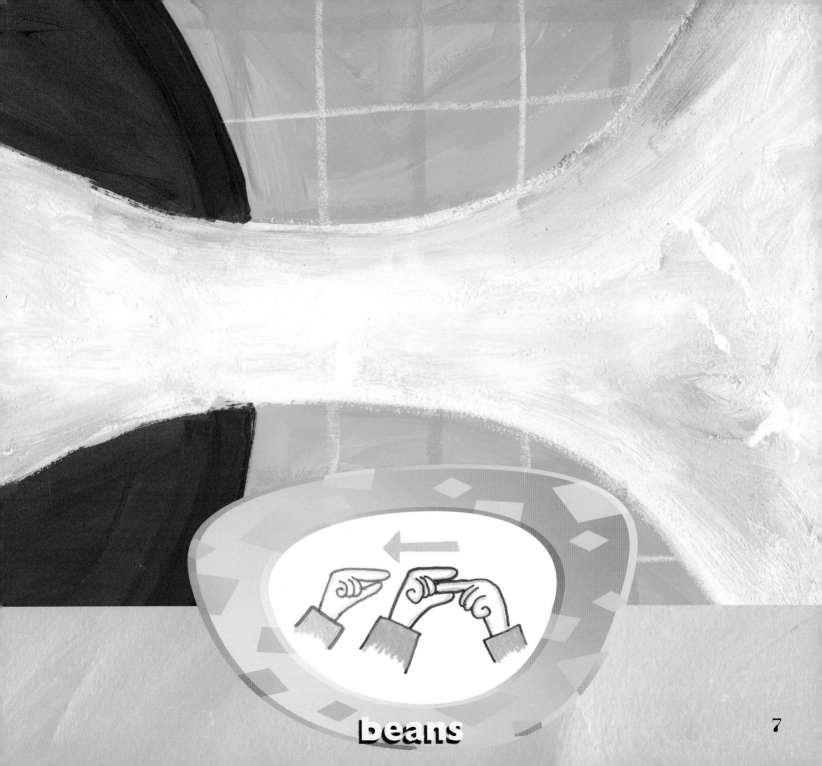

beans

Dog rolls **peas** into our bowl. They are the tiniest **peas** that you ever did see. The **peas** are on the beans in the big blue bowl.

"Fill it up, fill it up, fill it up," I say. And my friend Dog fills it up with me.

peas

Hen plops **corn** into our bowl. It is the juiciest **corn** that you ever did
see. The **corn** is on the peas that are on the beans in the big blue bowl.

"Fill it up, fill it up, fill it up," I say. And my friend Hen fills it up with me.

corn

Goat loads **squash** into our bowl. It is the heaviest **squash** that you ever did see. The **squash** is on the corn that's on the peas that're on the beans in the big blue bowl.

"Fill it up, fill it up, fill it up," I say. And my friend Goat fills it up with me.

squash

Pig dumps **rice** into our bowl. It is the fluffiest **rice** that you ever did see. The **rice** is on the squash that's on the corn that's on the peas that're on the beans in the big blue bowl.

"Fill it up, fill it up, fill it up," I say. And my friend Pig fills it up with me.

rice

Cat pours **milk** into our bowl. It is the creamiest **milk** that you ever did see. The **milk** is on the rice that's on the squash that's on the corn that's on the peas that're on the beans in the big blue bowl.

"Fill it up, fill it up, fill it up," I say. And my friend Cat fills it up with me.

16

milk

Mouse sprinkles **cheese** into our bowl. It is the curliest **cheese** that you ever did see. The **cheese** is on the milk that's on the rice, the squash, the corn, the peas, and the beans in the big blue bowl.

"Fill it up, fill it up, fill it up," I say. And my friend Mouse fills it up with me.

cheese

Bird breaks **bread** into our bowl. It is the crispiest **bread** that you ever did see. The **bread** is on the cheese, the milk, the rice, the squash, the corn, the peas, and the beans in the big blue bowl.

"Fill it up, fill it up, fill it up," I say. And my friend Bird fills it up with me.

bread

I drizzle **broth** into our bowl. It is the steamiest **broth** that you ever did see. The **broth** covers the bread, the cheese, the milk, the rice, the squash, the corn, the peas, and the beans in the big blue bowl.

"We filled it up, filled it up, filled it up," I say. My friends filled it up with me.

broth

There is stew in front of me. It is the jolliest stew that you ever did see. My friends stir it up, stir it up, stir it up with me. Then my friends serve it up, serve it up, serve it up with me. And my friends **slurp** it up, **slurp** it up, **slurp** it up with me.

slurp

Now all that's left is one big blue **bowl**. It is the emptiest **bowl** that you ever did see!

bowl

American Sign Language Glossary

 **bean:** Hold your hands in front of you and put your right "G Hand" around your left pointer finger. Now pull your right hand away from your left hand, and pinch your pointer finger and thumb together. Repeat this movement so it looks like you are showing the shape of a green bean.

 **bowl:** Hold your curved hands together in front of you with your palms facing up. Now move your hands out and up. It should look like you are outlining the shape of a bowl.

 **bread:** Put your left hand in front of you with your palm facing toward you like it is a loaf of bread. Now move the fingers of your right hand down the back of your left hand several times. It should look like you are slicing a loaf of bread.

 **broth:** *Use the sign for soup* by putting your left hand in front of you with your palm curved and facing up like it is a bowl. Now touch your right "U Hand" to the palm of your left hand and then to your mouth with a repeated movement. It should look like you are using a spoon to scoop up soup from a bowl.

 **cheese:** Hold your hands in front of you with the heel of your right hand resting in the palm of your left hand. Now, twist the heel of the right hand back and forth, keeping the right palm facing down. It should look like you are pressing the moisture out of a block of cheese.

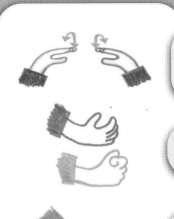

corn: Hold both flattened "C Hands" in front of your mouth with your palms facing each other. Now twist your hands forward and back. It should look like you are holding and eating corn-on-the-cob.

milk: Open and close your fist, alternating from a "C Hand" to an "S Hand." It should look like you are milking a cow.

pea: Hold your left pointer finger in front of you with your palm facing down. Now tap your right pointer finger along the back of your left pointer finger. It should look like you are counting the peas in a pea pod.

rice: Put your left hand in front of you with your palm curved and facing up like it is a bowl. Now touch your right "R Hand" to the palm of your left hand and then to your mouth. It should look like you are eating rice from a bowl.

slurp: *Use the sign for eat* by tapping the fingers of your flattened "O Hand" to your lips. It should look like you are putting food into your mouth.

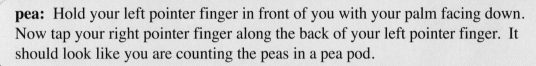

squash: Fingerspell S-Q-U-A-S-H.

Fun Facts about ASL

If you know you are going to repeat a fingerspelled word during a conversation or story, you can fingerspell it the first time, then quickly show a related ASL sign to use the next time. For example, you can fingerspell S-T-E-W, then sign soup. This shows your signing partner that you mean "stew" the next time you sign "soup."

Most sign language dictionaries describe how a sign looks for a right-handed signer. If you are left-handed, you would modify the instructions so the signs feel more comfortable to you. For example, to sign "pea," a left-handed signer would hold their right pointer finger in front of their body and tap with their left pointer finger.

Some signs use the handshape for the letter the word begins with to make the sign. These are called initialized signs. One example of an initialized sign is the word *rice*.

6 7 8 9 10

Signing Activities

 **Make a Sign Language Placemat:** Get a piece of construction paper, some old magazines, scissors, and paste. Cut out pictures from the magazines for six of your favorite food and drink items that you read in this book. Paste these pictures onto your construction paper. Draw pictures or write hints on the back of your placemat to help you remember the signs for the items on the front. Practice your signs at mealtime!

 **Lunchbox Learning:** Try this activity at mealtime. Look at the meal you are about to eat and make the sign for at least one item that you see. If you don't know the signs for any of the food or drink items in front of you, fingerspell at least one word that describes your meal. If you are eating with friends or family, go around the table and have each person sign one food or drink item. Bon appétit!

 **Read and Sign Circle Game**: List the words from the glossary on a poster, then get a group together and sit in a semicircle. Choose someone to be the reader. Assign a glossary word to everyone else in the group. As the story is read aloud, listeners should sign their glossary word each time it comes up in the story. Try it first with the reader reading at a normal pace. If that's too easy, assign new glossary words, and try it again with the reader reading at a faster pace. See how fast you can go without giggling!

Additional Resources

Further Reading

Costello, Elaine, PhD. *Random House Webster's Concise American Sign Language Dictionary*. Bantam, 2002.

Heller, Lora. *Sign Language for Kids*. Sterling, 2004.

Sign2Me. *Pick Me Up! Fun Songs for Learning Signs (A CD and Activity Guide)*. Northlight Communications, 2003.

Warner, Penny. *Signing Fun*. Gallaudet University Press, 2006.

Web Sites

To learn more about ASL, visit ABDO Group online at **www.abdopublishing.com**. Web sites about ASL are featured on our Book Links page. These links are routinely monitored and updated to provide the most current information available.